HAPPY BIRTH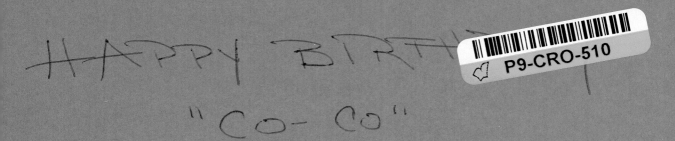

"CO-CO"

FROM YOUR NAUGHTY
Little Sister,

"LiBBET"

XO

My Naughty Little Sister Storybook

DOROTHY EDWARDS
Illustrated by Shirley Hughes

Clarion Books/New York

Clarion Books
a Houghton Mifflin Company imprint
215 Park Avenue South, New York, NY 10003

All these stories first appeared in:
My Naughty Little Sister © 1952 by Dorothy Edwards
More Naughty Little Sister Stories and
Some Others © 1957 by Dorothy Edwards
My Naughty Little Sister's Friends © 1962 by Dorothy Edwards
First published in this colored edition 1990
by Methuen Children's Books,
A Division of the Octopus Publishing Group
Michelin House, 81 Fulham Road, London, England SW3 6RB
Illustrations copyright © 1969 and 1990 by Shirley Hughes
Coloring of illustrations by Mark Burgess
Copyright © 1990 by Methuen Children's Books

Library of Congress Cataloging-in-Publication Data
Edwards, Dorothy.
My naughty little sister storybook / Dorothy Edwards : illustrated
by Shirley Hughes.
p.   cm.
Summary: Previously published stories assembled for this edition
feature the teller's rambunctious little sister, her family, and
friends.
ISBN 0-89919-857-0
1. Children's stories, English.   [1. Sisters—Fiction.   2. Family
life—Fiction.]   I. Hughes, Shirley, ill.   II. Title.
PZ7.E2518Mz   1991   90-2331
[E]—dc20   CIP
                                      AC

Contents

1. The naughtiest story of all   5

2. When my father minded   13
    my naughty little sister

3. The cross photograph   22

4. My naughty little sister   29
    and the big girl's bed

5. My naughty little sister and the sweep   36

6. Bad Harry's haircut   43

7. My naughty little sister at the party   49

8. My naughty little sister shows off   58

9. My naughty little sister   65
    is a curly girl

10. My naughty little sister cuts out   74

11. My naughty little sister   81
    and the workmen

12. The cross, spotty child   89

1. The naughtiest story of all

This is such a very terrible story about my naughty little sister that I hardly know how to tell it to you. It is all about one Christmas-time.

Now, my naughty little sister was very pleased when Christmas began to draw near, because she liked all the excitement of the plum-puddings and the turkeys, and the crackers and the holly, and all the Christmassy-looking shops, but there was one very awful thing about her – she didn't like to think about Father Christmas at all – she said he was a *horrid old man*!

There – I knew you would be shocked at that. But she did. And she said she wouldn't put up her stocking for him.

My mother told my naughty little sister what a good old man Father Christmas was, and how he brought the toys along on Christmas Eve, but my naughty little sister said, "I don't care. And I don't want that nasty old man coming to our house."

Well now, that was bad enough, wasn't it? But the really dreadful thing happened later on.

This is the dreadful thing: one day, my school-teacher said that a Father Christmas Man would be coming to the school to bring presents for all the children, and my teacher said that the Father Christmas Man would have toys for all our little brothers and sisters as well, if they cared to come along for them. She said that there would be a real Christmas-tree with candles on it, and sweeties and cups of tea and biscuits for our mothers.

Wasn't that a nice thought? Well now, when I told my little sister about the Christmas-tree, she said, "Oh, nice!"

And when I told her about the sweeties she said, "Very, very nice!" But when I told her about the Father Christmas Man, she said, "Don't want *him*, nasty old man."

Still, my mother said, "You can't go to the Christmas-tree without seeing him, so if you don't want to see him all that much, you will have to stay at home."

But my naughty little sister did want to go, very much, so she said, "I will go, and when the horrid Father Christmas Man comes in, I will close my eyes."

So, we all went to the Christmas-tree together, my mother, and I, and my naughty little sister.

When we got to the school, my naughty little sister was very pleased to see all the pretty paperchains that we had made in school hanging all round the classrooms, and when she saw all the little lanterns, and the holly and all the robin-redbreast drawings pinned on the blackboard she smiled and smiled. She was very smily at first.

All the mothers, and the little brothers and sisters who were too young for school, sat down in chairs and desks, and all the big schoolchildren acted a play for them.

My little sister was very excited to see all the children dressed up as fairies and robins and elves and Bo-peeps and things, and she clapped her hands very hard, like all the grown-ups did, to show that she was enjoying herself. And she still smiled.

Then, when some of the teachers came round with bags of sweets, tied up in pretty coloured paper, my little sister smiled even more, and she sang too when all the children sang. She sang, "Away in a manger," because she knew the words very well. When she didn't know the words of some of the singing, she "la-la'd".

After all the singing, the teachers put out the lights, and took away a big screen from a corner of the room, and there was the Christmas-tree, all lit up with candles and shining with silvery stuff, and little shiny coloured balls. There were lots of toys on the tree, and all the children cheered and clapped.

Then the teachers put the lights on again, and blew out the candles, so that we could all go and look at the tree. My little sister went too. She looked at the tree, and she looked at the toys, and she saw a specially nice doll with a blue dress on, and she said, "For me."

My mother said, "You must wait and see what you are given."

Then the teachers called out, "Back to your seats, everyone, we have a visitor coming." So all the children went back to their seats, and sat still and waited and listened.

And, as we waited and listened, we heard a tinkle-tinkle bell noise, and then the schoolroom door opened, and in walked the Father Christmas Man. My naughty little sister had forgotten all about him, so she hadn't time to close her eyes before he walked in. However, when she saw him, my little sister stopped smiling and began to be stubborn.

The Father Christmas Man was very nice. He said he hoped we were having a good time, and we all said,"Yes," except my naughty little sister – she didn't say a thing.

Then he said, "Now, one at a time, children; and I will give each one of you a toy."

So, first of all each schoolchild went up for a toy, and my naughty little sister still didn't shut her eyes because she wanted to see who was going to have the specially nice doll in the blue dress. But none of the schoolchildren had it.

Then Father Christmas began to call the little brothers and sisters up for presents, and, as he didn't know their names, he just said, "Come along, sonny," if it were a boy, and "come along, girlie," if it were a girl. The Father

Christmas Man let the little brothers and sisters choose their own toys off the tree.

When my naughty little sister saw this, she was so worried about the specially nice doll, that she thought that she would just go up and get it.

She said, "I don't like that horrid old beardy man, but I do like that nice doll."

So, my naughty little sister got up without being asked to, and she went right out to the front where the Father Christmas Man was standing, and she said, "That doll, please," and pointed to the doll she wanted.

The Father Christmas Man laughed and all the teachers laughed, and the other mothers and the schoolchildren, and all the little brothers and sisters. My mother did not laugh because she was so shocked to see my naughty little sister going out without being asked to.

The Father Christmas Man took the specially nice doll off the tree, and he handed it to my naughty little sister and he said, "Well now, I hear you don't like me very much, but won't you just shake hands?" and my naughty little sister said, "No." But she took the doll all the same.

The Father Christmas Man put out his nice old hand for her to shake and be friends, and do you know what that naughty bad girl did? *She bit his hand.* She really and truly

did. Can you think of anything more dreadful and terrible? She bit Father Christmas's good old hand, and then she turned and ran and ran out of the school with all the children staring after her, and her doll held very tight in her arms.

The Father Christmas Man was very nice. He said it wasn't a hard bite, only a frightened one, and he made all the children sing songs together.

When my naughty little sister was brought back by my mother, she said she was very sorry, and the Father Christmas Man said, "That's all right, old lady," and because he was so smily and nice to her, my funny little sister went right up to him, and gave him a big "sorry" kiss, which pleased him very much.

And she hung her stocking up after all, and that kind man remembered to fill it for her.

My little sister kept the specially nice doll until she was quite grown-up. She called it Rosy-primrose, and although she was sometimes bad-tempered with it, she really loved it very much indeed.

2. When my father minded my naughty little sister

My naughty little sister had a very cross friend. My little sister's cross friend was called Mr Blakey, and he was a very grumbly old man.

My little sister's friend Mr Blakey was the shoe-mender man, and he had a funny little shop with bits of leather all over the floor, and boxes of nails, and boot-polish, and shoe-laces, all over the place. Mr Blakey had a picture in his shop too. It was a very beautiful picture of a little dog with boots on all four feet, walking in the rain. My little sister loved that picture very much, but she loved Mr Blakey better than that.

Every time we went in Mr Blakey's shop with our mother, my naughty little sister would start meddling with things, and Mr Blakey would say, "Leave that be, you varmint," in a very loud, cross voice, and my little sister would stop meddling at once, just like an obedient child, because Mr Blakey was her favourite man; and one day, when we went into his shop, do you know what she did? She went straight behind the counter and kissed him without being asked. Mr Blakey was very surprised because he had a lot of nails in his mouth, but after that, he always gave her a peppermint humbug after he had shouted at her.

Well, that's about Mr Blakey, in case you wonder who he was later on. Now this is the real story.

One day, my mother had to go out shopping, so she asked my father if he would mind my naughty little sister for the day. My mother said she would take me shopping because I was a big girl, but my little sister was too draggy and moany to go to the big shops.

My father said he would mind my little sister, but my little sister said, "I want to go, I want to go." You know how she said that by now, I think. "I want to go" – like that. And she kicked and screamed.

My mother said, "Oh dear, how tiresome you are," to my little sister, but my father said, "You'll jolly well do as you're told, old lady."

Then my naughty little sister wouldn't eat her breakfast, but my mother went off shopping with me just the same,

and when we had gone, my father looked very fierce, and he said, "What about that breakfast?"

So my naughty little sister ate all her breakfast up, every bit, and she said, "More milk, please," and, "more bread, please," so much that my father got tired getting it for her.

Then, as it was a hot day, my father said, "I'll bring my work into the garden, and give an eye to you at the same time."

So my father took a chair and a table out into the garden, and my little sister went out into the garden too, and because my father was there she played good child's games. She didn't tread on the baby seedlings, or pick the flowers, or steal the blackcurrants, or do anything at all wicked. She didn't want my father to look fierce again, and my father said she was a good, nice child.

My little sister just sat on the lawn and played with Rosy-primrose, and she made a tea-party with leaves and nasturtium seeds, and when she wanted something she asked my father for it nicely, not going off and finding it for herself at all.

She said, "Please, Father, would you get me Rosy-primrose's box?" and my father put down his pen, and his writing paper, and got out of his chair, and went and got Rosy-primrose's box, which was on the top shelf of the toy-cupboard and had all Rosy-primrose's tatty old clothes in it.

Then my father did writing again, and then my little sister said, "Please can I have a drink of water?" She said it nicely. "Please," she said.

That was very good of her to ask, because sometimes she used to drink germy water out of the water-butt; but Father wasn't pleased at all, he said, "Bother!" because he was being a busy man, and he stamped and stamped to the kitchen to get the water for my polite little sister.

But my father didn't know about Rosy-primrose's water. You see, when my little sister had a drink she always gave Rosy-primrose a drink too in a blue doll's cup. So when my father brought back the water, my little sister said, "Where is Rosy-primrose's water?" and my cross father said, "Bother Rosy-primrose," like that, cross and grumbly.

And my father was crosser and grumblier when my little sister asked him to put Rosy-primrose's box back in the toy-cupboard. He said, "That wretched doll again?" and he took Rosy-primrose and shut her in the box too, and put it on top of the bookcase, to show how firm he was going to be. So then my little sister stopped being good.

She started to yell and stamp, and make such a noise that people going by looked over the hedge to see what the matter was. Wouldn't you have been ashamed if it were you stamping and yelling with people looking at you? My naughty little sister wasn't ashamed. *She* didn't care about the people at all; she was a stubborn bad child.

My father was a stubborn man too. He took his table and his chair and his writing things indoors, and shut himself away in his study.

"You'll jolly well stay there till you behave," he said to my naughty little sister.

My naughty little sister cried and cried until my father looked out of the window and said, "Any more of that, and off to bed you go." Then she was quiet, because she didn't want to go to bed.

She only peeped in once after that, but my father said, "Go away, do," and went on writing and writing, and he was so interested in his writing, he forgot all about my little sister, and it wasn't until he began to get hungry that he remembered her at all.

Then my father went out into the kitchen, and there was a lot of nice salad-stuff in the kitchen that our mother had left for lunch. There was junket, too, and stewed pears, and biscuits for my father's and my little sister's lunches. My father remembered my little sister then, and he went to call her for lunch, because it was quite late. It was so late it was four o'clock.

But my little sister wasn't in the garden. My father looked and looked. He looked among the marrows, and behind the runner-bean rows, and under the hedge. He looked in the shed and down the cellar-hole, but there was no little girl.

Then my father went indoors again and looked all over the house, and all the time he was calling and calling, but there was still no little girl at all.

Then my father got worried. He didn't stop to change his slippers or eat his lunch. He went straight out of the gate, and down the road to look for my little sister. But he couldn't see her at all. He asked people, "Have you seen a little girl with red hair?" and people said, "No."

My father was just coming up the road again, looking so hot and so worried, when my mother and I got off the bus.

When my mother saw him, she said, "He's lost that child," because she knows my father and my little sister rather well.

When we got indoors my mother said, "Why haven't you eaten your lunch?" and then my father told her all about the writing, and my bad sister. So my mother said, "Well, if she's anywhere, she's near food of some kind.

Have you looked in the larder?" My father said he had. So Mother said, "Well, I don't know –"

Then I said something clever. I said, "I expect she is with old Mr Blakey." So we went off to Mr Blakey's shop, and there she was. Fast asleep on a pile of leather bits.

Mr Blakey seemed quite cross with us for having lost her, and my naughty little sister was very cross when we took her away because she said she had had a lovely time with Mr Blakey. Mr Blakey had boiled her an egg in his tea-kettle, and given her some bread and cheese out of newspaper, and let her cut it for herself with one of his nice leathery knives. Mother was cross because she had been looking forward to a nice cup of tea after the bus journey, and I was cross because my little sister had had such a fine time in Mr Blakey's shop.

The only happy one was my father. He said, "Thank goodness I can work again without having to concentrate on a disagreeable baby." However, that made my little sister cry again, so he wasn't happy for long.

3. The cross photograph

A long time ago, my mother made my naughty little sister and me a beautiful coat each.

They were lovely red coats with black buttons to do them up with and curly-curly black fur on them to keep us warm. We were very proud children when we put our new red coats on.

Our mother was proud too, because she had never made any coats before, and she said, "I know! You shall have your photographs taken. Then we can always remember how smart they look."

So our proud mother took my naughty little sister and me to have our photographs taken in our smart red coats.

The man in the photographer's shop was very smart too. He had curly-curly black hair *just* like the fur on our new coats, and he had a pink flower in his buttonhole and a yellow handkerchief that he waved and waved when he took our photographs.

There were lots of pictures in the shop. There were pictures of children, and ladies being married, and ladies smiling, and gentlemen smiling, and pussy-cats with long fur, and black-and-white rabbits. All those pictures! And the smart curly-curly man had taken every one himself!

He said we could go and look at his pictures while he talked to our mother, so I went round and looked at them. But do you know, my naughty little sister wouldn't look. She stood still as still and quiet as quiet, and she shut her eyes.

Yes, she did. She shut her eyes and wouldn't look at anything. She was being a stubborn girl, and when the photographer-man said, "Are you both ready?" my bad little sister kept her eyes shut and said, *"No."*

Our mother said, "But surely you want your photograph taken?"

But my naughty little sister kept her eyes shut tight as tight, and said, "No taken! No taken!" And she got so cross, and shouted so much, that the curly man said, "All right then. I will just take your big sister by herself."

"I will take a nice photograph of your big sister," said the photographer-man, "and she will be able to show it to all her friends. Wouldn't you like a photograph of yourself to show to your friends?"

My naughty little sister did want a photograph of herself to show to her friends, but she would not say so. She just said, "No photograph!"

So our mother said, "Oh well, it looks as if it will be only one picture then, for we can't keep this gentleman waiting all day."

So the photographer-man made me stand on a box-thing. There was a little table on the box-thing, and I had to put my hand on the little table and stand up straight and smile.

There was a beautiful picture of a garden on the wall behind me. It was such a big picture that when the photograph was taken it looked just as if I was standing in a real garden. Wasn't that a clever idea?

When I was standing quite straight and quite smily, the curly photographer-man shone a lot of bright lights, and then he got his big black camera-on-legs and said, "Watch for the dicky-bird!" And he waved and waved his yellow handkerchief. And then "Click!" said the camera, and my picture was safe inside it.

"That's all," said the man, and he helped me to get down.

Now, what do you think? While the man was taking my picture, my little sister had opened her eyes to peep, and when she saw me standing all straight and smily in my beautiful new coat, and heard the man say, "Watch for the dicky-bird," and saw him wave his yellow handkerchief, she stared and stared.

The man said, "That was all right, wasn't it?" and I said, "Yes, thank you."

Then the curly man looked at my little sister and he saw that her eyes weren't shut any more so he said, "Are you going to change your mind now?"

And what do you think? My little sister changed her mind. She stopped being stubborn. She changed her mind and said, "Yes, please," like a good polite child. You see, she hadn't known anything about photographs before, and she had been frightened, but when she saw me having my picture taken, and had seen how easy it was, she hadn't been frightened any more.

She let the man lift her on to the box-thing. She was so small though, that he took the table away and found a little chair for her to sit on, and gave her a teddy-bear to hold.

Then he said, "Smile nicely now," and my naughty little sister smiled very beautifully indeed.

The man said, "Watch for the dicky-bird," and he waved his yellow handkerchief to her, and "click", my naughty little sister's photograph had been taken too!

But what do you think? She hadn't kept smiling. When the photographs came home for us to look at, there was my little sister holding the teddy-bear and looking as cross as cross.

Our mother *was* surprised; she said, "I thought the man

told you to *smile*!"

And what do you think that funny girl said? She said,
"I did smile, but there wasn't any dicky-bird, so I stopped."

My mother said, "Oh dear! We shall have to have it
taken all over again!"

But our father said, "No, I like this one. It is such a
natural picture. I like it as it is." And he laughed and
laughed and laughed and laughed.

The cross photograph

My little sister liked the cross picture very much too, and sometimes, when she hadn't anything else to do, she climbed up to the looking-glass and made cross faces at herself. *Just* like the cross face in the photograph!

4. My naughty little sister and the big girl's bed

A long time ago, my naughty little sister had a nice cot with pull-up sides so that she couldn't fall out and bump herself.

My little sister's cot was a very pretty one. It was pink, and had pictures of fairies and bunny-rabbits painted on it.

It had been my old cot when I was a very small child and I had taken care of the pretty pictures. I used to kiss the fairies 'good night' when I went to bed, but my bad little sister did not kiss them and take care of their pictures. Oh no!

My naughty little sister did dreadful things to those poor fairies. She scribbled on them with pencils and scratched them with tin-lids, and knocked them with poor old Rosy-primrose, her doll, until there were hardly any pictures left at all. She said, "Nasty fairies. Silly old rabbits."

There! Wasn't she a bad child? You wouldn't do things like that, would you?

And my little sister jumped and jumped on her cot. After she had been tucked up at night-time she would get out from under the covers, and jump and jump. And when she woke up in the morning she jumped and jumped again, until one day, when she was jumping, the bottom fell right out of the cot, and my naughty little sister, and the mattress, and the covers, and poor Rosy-primrose all fell out on to the floor!

Then our mother said, "That child must have a bed!" Even though our father managed to mend the cot, our mother said, "She must have a bed!"

My naughty little sister said, "A big bed for me?"

And our mother said, "I am afraid so, you bad child. You are too rough now for your poor old cot."

My little sister wasn't ashamed of being too rough for her cot. She was pleased because she was going to have the new bed, and she said, "A big girl's bed for me!"

My little sister told everybody that she was going to have a big girl's bed. She told her kind friend the window-cleaner man, and the coalman, and the milkman.

She told the dustman too. She said, "You can have my old cot soon, dustman, because I am going to have a big girl's bed." And she was as pleased as pleased.

But our mother wasn't pleased at all. She was rather worried. You see, our mother was afraid that my naughty little sister would jump and jump on her new bed, and scratch it, and treat it badly. My naughty little sister had done such dreadful things to her old cot, that my mother was afraid she would spoil the new bed too.

Well now, my little sister told the lady who lived next door all about her new bed. The lady who lived next door to us was called Mrs Jones, but my little sister used to call her Mrs Cocoa Jones because she used to go in and have a cup of cocoa with her every morning.

Mrs Cocoa Jones was a very kind lady, and when she heard about the new bed she said, "I have a little yellow eiderdown and a yellow counterpane upstairs, and they are too small for any of my beds, so when your new bed comes, I will give them to you."

My little sister was excited, but when she told our mother what Mrs Cocoa had said, our mother shook her head.

"Oh dear," she said, "what will happen to the lovely eiderdown and counterpane when our bad little girl has them?"

Then a kind aunt who lived near us said, "I have a dear little green nightie-case put away in a drawer. It belonged to me when I was a little girl. When your new bed comes you can have it to put your nighties in like a big girl."

My little sister said, "Good. Good," because of all the nice things she was going to have for her bed. But our mother was more worried than ever. She said, "Oh dear! That pretty nightie-case. You'll spoil it, I know you will!"

But my little sister went on being pleased as pleased about it.

Then one day the new bed arrived. It was a lovely, shiny brown bed, new as new, with a lovely blue stripy mattress to go on it, new as new. And there was a new stripy pillow too. Just like a real big girl would have.

My little sister watched while my mother took the poor old cot to pieces, and stood it up against the wall. She watched when the new bed was put up, and the new mattress was laid on top of it. She watched the new pillow being put into a clean white case, and when our mother made the bed with clean new sheets and clean new blankets, she said, "Really big-girl! A big girl's bed – all for me."

Then Mrs Cocoa Jones came in, and she was carrying the pretty yellow eiderdown and the yellow counterpane. They were very shiny and satiny like buttercup flowers, and when our mother put them on top of the new bed, they looked beautiful.

Then our kind aunt came down the road, and *she* was carrying a little parcel, and in the little parcel was the pretty green nightie-case. My little sister ran down the road to meet her because she was so excited. She was more excited still when our aunt picked up her little nightdress and put it into the pretty green case and laid the green case on the yellow shiny eiderdown.

My little sister was so pleased that she was glad when bedtime came.

And, what do you think? She got carefully, carefully into bed with Rosy-primrose, and she laid herself down and stretched herself out – carefully, carefully like a good, nice girl.

And she didn't jump and jump, and she didn't scratch the shiny brown wood, or scribble with pencils or scrape with tin-lids. Not ever! Not even when she had had the new bed a long, long time.

My little sister took great care of her big girl's bed. She took great care of her shiny yellow eiderdown and counterpane and her pretty green nightie-case.

And whatever do you think she said to me?

She said, "You had the fairy pink cot before I did. But this is my very own big girl's bed, and I am going to take great care of my very own bed, like a big girl!"

5. *My naughty little sister and the sweep*

One morning when my naughty little sister and I went downstairs to breakfast we found everything looking very funny indeed.

The table was pushed right up against the wall, and the chairs were standing on the table and they were all covered over with a big sheet. The curtains were gone from the window, and the armchairs and the pictures and the clock and lots of other things. All gone!

My little sister was very interested to see all this, and when she looked out of the window, she saw that the armchairs and the pictures and all the other things were piled up in our back garden. My little sister *did* stare.

Clock and pictures and armchairs in the back garden, and things covered up with sheets; no curtains! Wasn't that a strange thing to find? My little sister said, "We have

36

got a funny home today."

Then my mother told us that the chimney-sweep was coming to clean the chimney and that she had had to get the room ready for him. My naughty little sister was very excited because she had never seen a sweep, and she jumped and said, "Sweep," and jumped and said, "Sweep," again and again because she was so excited. Then she said, "Won't we have any breakfast?"

"Won't we have any breakfast?" said my hungry little sister, because the chairs were standing on the table. And Mother said, "As it is a lovely sunny morning you are going to have a picnic breakfast in the garden."

Then my little sister was very pleased indeed because she had never had a picnic breakfast before.

She said, "What shall we eat?" and my mother told her, "Well, as it is a special picnic breakfast, I have made you some egg sandwiches." Wasn't that nice? Sandwiches for breakfast! There was milk too, and bananas. My sister *did* like it!

We sat on the back doorstep and ate and ate and drank and drank because it was so nice to be eating our breakfast in the open air.

Then, just as my little sister finished her very last bite of banana, a big man with a black-dirty face came in the back gate and Mother said, "Here is the sweep at last."

Well, *you* know all about sweeps, but my little sister didn't, and she was so interested that my mother said she could watch the sweep so long as she didn't meddle in any way. My sister said she would be very good, so my mother found her one of my overalls, and tied a hanky round her head to keep her hair clean, and said, "Now you can go and watch the sweep."

My little sister watched the sweep man push the brush up the chimney and she watched when he screwed a cane

on to the brush and a cane on to that cane, and a cane on to that cane, all the time pushing the brush up and up the chimney, and she stayed as good as good. She was very quiet. She didn't say a thing.

She was so mousy-quiet that the black sweep man said, "You are quiet, missy; haven't you got a tongue?"

My sister was very surprised when the sweep asked if she had got a tongue, so she stuck her tongue out quickly to show that she had got one, and he said, "Fancy that now!"

Then my little sister laughed and the sweep laughed and she wasn't quiet any more. She talked and talked until he had finished his work.

Then my sister asked the sweep what he was going to do with all the soot he had collected and he said, "I shall leave it for your father to use in his garden. It's good for frightening off the tiddy little slugs."

So, when the sweep man went away he left a little pile of soot in the garden for our father. My sister was sorry when he went away, and she asked my mother lots of questions. She wanted to know so many things that Mother said, "If I answer you now I'll never get the place straight, so just you run off and play like a good girl, and I will tell you all about soot and chimney-sweeps later on."

So my sister went off, and Mother cleaned up the room and brought in the chairs and hung up the curtains and did all the other tidying up things and all the time my sister was very quiet.

There had been lots of things my sister had wanted to know very badly. One thing she had wanted to know was if there was soot in *all* the chimneys. She wondered if there was any soot in her own bedroom chimney.

She went upstairs and looked up her chimney but she couldn't see because it was too dark up there.

It was very dark and my sister probably wouldn't have bothered any more about it, only she happened to remember that there was a long cane on the landing with a feather duster on the top, that Mother used for getting the cobwebs from the top of the stairs.

Yes, I thought you would guess. The cane was very bendy and it wasn't difficult for a little girl to push it up the chimney.

Have you ever done anything so very silly as this? If you have you will know how dirty soot is. It's much dirtier than mud even.

My silly sister pushed the feather duster up her bedroom chimney and a lot of soot fell down into the fireplace. It was such a lot of soot and it looked so dirty

that my little sister got frightened and wished that she hadn't done such an awful thing.

She couldn't help thinking that Mother would be very cross when she saw it.

So she thought she had better hide it.

You will never guess where that silly child tried to hide the soot. *In her bed*.

Yes, in her own nice clean little comfortable bed.

I'm glad to think that you wouldn't be so silly.

My sister made such a mess carrying the soot across the room and touching things with her sooty fingers and treading on the floor with sooty feet that she didn't know what to do.

She saw how messy her bedroom was and she was very, very sorry; she was so sorry that she ran right downstairs to the garden where Mother was shaking the mats, and she flung her little sooty arms round Mother's skirt, and pushed her little sooty face into Mother's apron, and she said, "Oh, I have been a bad girl. I have been a bad girl. Scold me a lot. Scold me a lot." And then she cried and cried and cried and cried and *cried*.

And she was so sorry and so ashamed that Mother forgave her even though it made her a lot of extra work on a very busy day.

My little sister was so sorry that she fetched things and carried things and told Mother when the sheets were dry and helped to lay the table for dinner and behaved like the best child in England, so that our father said it was almost worth having her behave so badly when she could show afterwards what a good girl she really was.

Our father was a very funny man.

6. Bad Harry's haircut

Bad Harry was a little boy who only lived a little way away from us, and as there were no nasty roads to cross between our houses, he used to come all on his own to play with my little sister, and she used to go all on her own to play with him. And they were Very Good Friends.

And they were both very naughty children. Oh dear!

But if you could have seen this Bad Harry you wouldn't have said that he was a naughty child. He looked so very good. Yes, he looked very good indeed.

My little sister never looked very good, even when she was behaving herself, but Bad Harry looked good all the time.

My naughty little sister's friend Harry had big, big blue eyes and pretty golden curls like a baby angel, but oh dear, he was quite naughty all the same.

Now one day, when my little sister went round to play with Harry, she found him looking very smart indeed. He was wearing real big boy's trousers. Real ones, with real big boy's buttons and real big boy's braces! Red braces like a very big boy! Wasn't he smart?

"Look," said Bad Harry. "Look at my big boy's trousers."

"Smart," said my naughty little sister, "smart boy."

"I'm going to have a real boy's haircut too," said Bad Harry. "Today. Not Mummy with scissors any more; but a real boy's haircut in a real barber's shop!"

My word, he was a proud boy!

My little sister was *so* surprised, and Bad Harry was *so* pleased to see how surprised she was.

"I'll be a big boy then," he said.

Then Harry's mother, who was a kind lady and liked my little sister very much, said that if she was a good girl she could come to the barber's and see Harry have his haircut.

My little sister was so excited that she ran straight back home at once to tell our mother all about Harry's big boy's trousers and Harry's real boy's haircut.

"Can I go too, can I go too?" she asked our mother.

Our mother said, "Yes, you may go, only hold very tight to Harry's mother's hand when you cross the High Street," and my little sister promised that she would hold

very tight indeed.

So off they went to the barber's to get Harry a Real Boy's Haircut.

My little sister had never been in a barber's shop before and she stared and stared. Bad Harry had never been in a barber's shop before either, but he didn't stare; he pretended that he knew all about it. He picked up one of the barber's books and pretended to look at the pictures in it, but he peeped all the time at the barber's shop.

There were three haircut-men in the barber's shop, and

they all had white coats and they all had black combs sticking out of their pockets.

There were three white wash-basins with shiny taps and looking-glasses, and three very funny chairs. In the three funny chairs were three men all having something done to them by the three haircut-men.

One man was having his hair cut with scissors, and one man was having his neck clipped with clippers, and one man had a soapy white face and *he* was being shaved!

And there were bottles and bottles, and brushes and brushes, and towels and towels, and pretty pictures with writing on them, and all sorts of things to see! My little sister looked and Bad Harry peeped until it was Harry's turn to have his hair cut.

When it was Harry's turn one of the haircut-men fetched a special high-chair for Harry to sit in, because the grown-up chairs were all too big.

Harry sat in the special chair and then the haircut-man got a big blue sheet and wrapped it round Harry and tucked it in at the neck.

"You don't want any tickly old hairs going down there," the haircut-man said.

Then the haircut-man took his sharp shiny scissors and began to cut and cut. And down fell a golden curl and

"Gone!" said my little sister, and down fell another golden curl and, "Gone!" said my little sister again, and she said "Gone!" "Gone!" "Gone!" all the time until Harry's curls had quite gone away.

Then she said, "All gone now!"

When the haircut-man had finished cutting, he took a bottle with a squeezer-thing and he squirted some nice smelly stuff all over Harry's head and made Harry laugh, and my little sister laughed as well.

Then the haircut-man took the big black comb, and he made a Big Boy's Parting on Harry's head, and he combed

Harry's hair back into a real boy's haircut, and then Bad Harry climbed down from the high-chair so that my little sister could really look at him.

And then my little sister *did* stare. Bad Harry's mother stared too . . .

For there was that bad boy Harry, with his real boy's trousers and his real boy's braces, with a real boy's haircut, smiling and smiling, and looking very pleased.

"No curls now," said Bad Harry. "Not any more."

"No curls," said my naughty little sister.

"No," Bad Harry's mother said, "and oh dear! you don't even *look* good any more."

Then my little sister laughed and laughed. "Bad Harry!" she said. "Bad Harry. All bad now – like me!"

7. My naughty little sister at the party

You wouldn't think there could be another child as naughty as my naughty little sister, would you? But there was. There was a thoroughly bad boy who was my naughty little sister's best boy-friend: Bad Harry.

This Bad Harry and my naughty little sister used to play together quite a lot in Harry's garden, or in our garden, and got up to dreadful mischief between them, picking all the baby gooseberries, and the green blackcurrants, and throwing sand on the flower-beds, and digging up the runner-bean seeds, and all the naughty sorts of things you never, never do in the garden.

Now, one day this Bad Harry's birthday was near, and Bad Harry's mother said he could have a birthday-party and invite lots of children to tea. So Bad Harry came round to our house with a pretty card in an envelope for my naughty little sister, and this card was an invitation asking my naughty little sister to come to the birthday-party.

Bad Harry told my naughty little sister that there would be a lovely tea with jellies and sandwiches and birthday-cake, and my naughty little sister said, "Jolly good."

And every time she thought about the party she said, "Nice tea and birthday-cake." Wasn't she greedy? And when the party-day came she didn't make any fuss when my mother dressed her in her new green party-dress, and her green party-shoes and her green hair-ribbon, and she didn't fidget and she didn't wriggle her head about when she was having her hair combed, she kept as still as still, because she was so pleased to think about the party, and when my mother said, "Now, what must you say at the party?" my naughty little sister said, "I must say, 'nice tea'."

But my mother said, "No, no, that *would* be a greedy thing to say. You must say 'please' and 'thank you' like a good polite child, at tea-time, and say, 'thank you very much for having me,' when the party is over."

And my naughty little sister said, "All right, Mother, I promise."

So my mother took my naughty little sister to the party, and what do you think the silly little girl did as soon as she got there? She went up to Bad Harry's mother and she said very quickly, "Please-and-thank-you, and-thank-you-very-much-for-having-me," all at once – just like that, before she forgot to be polite, and then she said, "Now, may I have a lovely tea?"

Wasn't that rude and greedy? Bad Harry's mother said, "I'm afraid you will have to wait until all the other children are here, but Harry shall show you the tea-table if you like."

Bad Harry looked very smart in a blue party-suit, with white socks and shoes and a real boy's haircut, and he said, "Come on, I'll show you."

So they went into the tea-room and there was the birthday-tea spread out on the table. Bad Harry's mother had made red jellies and yellow jellies, and blancmanges and biscuits and sandwiches and cakes-with-cherries-on, and a big birthday-cake with white icing on it and candles, and "Happy Birthday, Harry" written on it.

My naughty little sister's eyes grew bigger and bigger, and Bad Harry said, "There's something else in the larder. It's going to be a surprise treat, but you shall see it because you are my best girl-friend."

So Bad Harry took my naughty little sister out into the kitchen and they took chairs and climbed up to the larder shelf – which is a dangerous thing to do, and it would have been their own faults if they had fallen down – and Bad Harry showed my naughty little sister a lovely spongy trifle, covered with creamy stuff and with silver balls and jelly-sweets on the top. And my naughty little sister stared more than ever because she liked spongy trifle better than jellies or blancmanges or biscuits or sandwiches or cakes-with-cherries-on, or even birthday-cake, so she said, "For me."

Bad Harry said, "For me too," because he liked spongy trifle best as well.

Then Bad Harry's mother called to them and said,

"Come along, the other children are arriving."

So they went to say, "How do you do!" to the other children, and then Bad Harry's mother said, "I think we will have a few games now before tea – just until everyone has arrived."

All the other children stood in a ring and Bad Harry's mother said, "Ring O'Roses first, I think." And all the nice party children said, "Oh, we'd like that."

But my naughty little sister said, "No Ring O'Roses – nasty Ring O'Roses" – just like that, because she didn't like Ring O'Roses very much, and Bad Harry said, "Silly game."

So Bad Harry and my naughty little sister stood and watched the others. The other children sang beautifully too, they sang,

"Ring O'Ring O'Roses,
A pocket full of posies –
A-tishoo, a-tishoo, we all fall down."

And they all fell down and laughed, but Harry and my naughty little sister didn't laugh. They got tired of watching and they went for a little walk. Do you know where they went to?

Yes. To the larder. To take another look at the spongy trifle. They climbed up on to the chairs to look at it really properly. It was very pretty.

"Ring O'Ring O'Roses," sang the good party children.

"Nice jelly-sweets," said my naughty little sister. "Nice silver balls," and she looked at that terribly Bad Harry and he looked at her.

"Take one," said that naughty boy, and my naughty little sister did take one, she took a red jelly-sweet from the top of the trifle; and then Bad Harry took a green jelly-

sweet; and then my naughty little sister took a yellow
jelly-sweet and a silver ball, and then Bad Harry took
three jelly-sweets, red, green and yellow, and six silver
balls, one, two, three, four, five, six, and put them all in
his mouth at once.

Now some of the creamy stuff had come off upon Bad
Harry's fingers and he liked it very much, so he put his
finger into the creamy stuff on the trifle, and took some of
it off and ate it, and my naughty little sister ate some too.
I'm sorry to have to tell you this, because I feel so ashamed

of them, and expect you feel ashamed of them too.

I hope you aren't too shocked to hear any more? Because, do you know, those two bad children forgot all about the party and the nice children all singing "Ring O'Roses". They took a spoon each and scraped off the creamy stuff and ate it, and then they began to eat the nice spongy inside.

Bad Harry said, "Now we've made the trifle look so untidy, no one else will want any, so we may as well eat it all up." So they dug away into the spongy inside of the trifle and found lots of nice fruity bits inside. It was a very big trifle, but those greedy children ate and ate.

Then, just as they had nearly finished the whole big trifle, the 'Ring O'Roses'-ing stopped, and Bad Harry's mother called, "Where are you two? We are ready for tea."

Then my naughty little sister was very frightened. Because she knew she had been very naughty, and she looked at Bad Harry and *he* knew *he* had been very naughty, and they both felt terrible. Bad Harry had a creamy mess of trifle all over his face, and even in his real boy's haircut, and my naughty little sister had made her new green party-dress all trifly – you know how it happens if you eat too quickly and greedily.

"It's tea-time," said Bad Harry, and he looked at my

naughty little sister, and my naughty little sister thought of the jellies and the cakes and the sandwiches, and all the other things, and she felt very full of trifle, and she said, "Don't want any."

And do you know what she did? Just as Bad Harry's mother came into the kitchen, my naughty little sister slipped out of the door, and ran and ran all the way home. It was a good thing our home was only down the street and no roads to cross, or I don't know what would have happened to her.

Bad Harry's mother was so cross when she saw the trifle, that she sent Bad Harry straight to bed, and he had to stay there and hear all the nice children enjoying themselves. I don't know what happened to him in the night, but I know that my naughty little sister wasn't at all a well girl, from having eaten so much trifle – and I also know that she doesn't like spongy trifle any more.

8. My naughty little sister shows off

Do you like climbing? My naughty little sister used to like climbing very much indeed. She climbed up fences and on chairs and down ditches and round railings, and my mother used to say, "One day that child will fall and hurt herself."

But our father said, "She will be all right if she is careful."

And my little sister *was* careful. She didn't want to hurt herself. She climbed on *easy things*, and when she knew she had gone far enough, she always came down again, slowly, slowly, carefully, carefully – one foot down – the other foot down – like that.

My little sister was so careful about climbing that our father nailed a piece of wood on to our front gate, so that she would have something to stand on when she wanted to look over it. There was a tree by the gate, and Father put an iron handle on the tree to help her to hold on tight. Wasn't he a kind daddy?

Well now, one day my naughty little sister went down to the front gate because she thought it would be nice to see all the people going by.

She climbed up carefully, carefully, like a good girl, and she held on to the iron handle, and she watched all the people going down the street.

First the postman came along. He said, "Hello, Monkey," and that made her laugh. She said, "Hello, postman, have you any letters for this house?" and the postman said, "Not today, I'm afraid, Monkey."

My little sister laughed again because the postman called her "Monkey", but she remembered to hold on tight.

Then Mr Cocoa Jones went by on his bicycle. Mr Cocoa said, "Don't fall," and he ling-a-linged his bicycle bell at her. "Be very careful," said Mr Cocoa Jones' bell.

My naughty little sister said, "I won't fall. I won't fall, Mr Cocoa. I'm sensible," and Mr Cocoa ling-a-linged his bell again and called "Good-bye".

My naughty little sister waved to Mr Cocoa. She waved very carefully. She didn't lean forward to see him go round the corner or anything silly like that. No, she was most careful.

She was careful when the nice baker came with the
bread. She climbed down, carefully, carefully and let him
in.

She was careful when cars went by. She held tight and
stood very still. She saw a steam-roller and a rag-a'-bone
man, and she held very tight indeed.

Then my naughty little sister saw her friend, Bad Harry,
coming down the road, and she forgot to be sensible.

She began to show off.

My little sister shouted, "Harry, Harry, look at me. I'm on the gate, Harry."

Bad Harry did look at her, because she called in such a loud voice, "Look at me!" like that.

Then my silly little sister stood on one leg only – just because she wanted Bad Harry to think she was a clever girl.

That made Bad Harry laugh, so my little sister showed off again. She stood on the other leg only, and then – she let go of the tree and waved her arms.

And then – she fell right off the gate. Bump! She fell down and bumped her head.

Oh dear! Her head *did* hurt, and my poor little sister cried and cried. Bad Harry cried too, and my mother came hurrying out of the house to see what had happened.

Our dear mother said, "Don't cry, don't cry, baby," in a kind, kind voice. "Don't cry, baby dear," she said, and she picked my little sister up and took her indoors and Bad Harry followed them. They were still crying and crying.

They cried so much that my mother gave them each a sugar lump to suck. Then they stopped crying because they found that they couldn't cry and suck at the same time.

Then our mother looked at my sister's poor head. "What a nasty bruise," our mother said. "I think I had better put something on it for you, and you must be a good brave girl while I do it."

My little sister was a good brave girl, too. She held Bad Harry's hand very tight, and she shut her eyes while Mother put some stingy stuff out of a bottle on to her poor head. Our mother did it very quickly, and my brave sister didn't fidget and she didn't cry. Wasn't she good?

When our mother had finished she gave my little sister and her friend, Bad Harry, an apple each and they went into the garden to play.

They had a lovely time playing in the garden. First they picked dandelions and put them in the water-tub for boats. Then they played hide-and-seek among the cabbages. Then they made a little house underneath the apple-tree. Then they found some blue chalk and drew funny old men on the tool-shed door.

And my little sister forgot all about her poor head.

When our father came home and saw my naughty little sister playing in the garden he said, "Hello, old lady, have you been in the wars?" and my little sister was surprised because she had forgotten all about falling off the gate. Father said, "You have got a nasty lump on top!"

So my little sister thought she would go indoors and look at her nasty lump. She climbed up on to a chair to look at herself in the mirror on the kitchen wall, and she saw that there was a big bump on her forehead. It was all yellowy-greeny.

Our mother said, "Climbing again! I should think you

would have had enough climbing for one day!"

My little sister looked at her big bump in the mirror, and then she climbed down from the chair, carefully, carefully.

She climbed down very carefully indeed, and do you know what she said? She said, "I like climbing very much, but I don't like falling down. And I *certainly* don't like nasty bumps on my head. So I don't think I will be a showing off girl any more."

9. *My naughty little sister is a curly girl*

Winnie, the little girl who used to come and see us sometimes when I was a little girl with a naughty little sister, was a very quiet, tidy child. She never rushed about and shouted or played dirty games, and she always wore neat clean dresses.

Winnie had some of those long round and round curls like chimney-pots that hung round her head in a very tidy way, and when Winnie moved her head these little curls jumped up and down. Mother told us that these curls were called ringlets.

One day, when Winnie and her mother were spending the afternoon at our house, my sister sat staring very hard at Winnie's ringlets, and all of a sudden she got up and went over to her and pushed one of her little fingers into one of Winnie's tidy ringlets.

Then, because the ringlet looked so nice on her finger, she pushed another finger into another ringlet.

Now, if anyone had interfered with my sister's hair she would have screamed and screamed – she even made a fuss when our mother brushed it – but Winnie sat still and quiet in a very mousy way, although I don't think she liked having her hair meddled with any more than my sister would have done.

Winnie's mother certainly didn't like it, and she said in a polite firm voice, "Please don't fiddle with Winifred's hair, dear; the curls may come out."

Then Winnie's mother said to our mother, "They take such ages to put in every night."

When Winnie's mother said this, my funny sister

thought that the curls would come right out of Winnie's head if she touched them too much. And she thought that Winnie's mother would have to pick all the curls up and put them back into Winnie's head at night-time. So she stopped touching Winnie's hair at once, and went and sat down again.

She didn't think she would like to be Winnie with falling-out curls.

My little sister sat looking at Winnie though, in case a curl should fall out on its own, but when it didn't, she got tired of looking at her, and went out into the garden instead to talk over the fence to dear Mrs Cocoa Jones.

"Mrs Cocoa," she said, "Winnie has funny curls."

Mrs Cocoa was surprised when my sister said this, so she told her what Winnie's mother had said about the curls coming out.

Now, Mrs Cocoa was a kind polite lady and she didn't laugh at my little sister for making such a funny mistake. She just told her all about how Winnie's mother made Winnie's curls for her.

Mrs Cocoa told my sister how, when *she* was a little girl, her kind old grandmother had curled *her* hair. She said that her grandmother had made her hair damp with a wet brush and had twisted her hair up in little pieces of rag, and how she had gone to bed with her hair twisted up like this and how, next morning, when her grandmother had undone her curlers she had had ringlets just like Winnie's.

My sister was very interested to hear all this.

"Of course," Mrs Cocoa said, "my granny only did up my hair on Saturday nights so that it would be curly for Sunday. On ordinary week-nights I had two little pigtails like yours."

When my sister heard Mrs Cocoa saying about how her grandmother curled her hair for her, she began to smile as big as that.

"I know, Mrs Cocoa," she said, "you can make me a curly girl."

Mrs Cocoa said that my sister would have to sit still and not scream then, and my sister said she would be very still indeed, so Mrs Cocoa said, "Well then, if your mother is willing, I'll pop in tonight and put some curlers in for you."

After that, my sister went back into the house, and sat very quietly looking at Winnie and Winnie's beautiful ringlets and smiling in a pussy-cat pleased way to herself.

She didn't say anything to Winnie and her mother about what kind Mrs Cocoa was going to do, but when they had gone she told Mother and me all about it, and Mother said it was very kind of Mrs Cocoa to offer to make ringlets of

my sister's hair, and she said, "Mrs Cocoa can try anyway, although I can't think *how* you will sit still without making a fuss."

But my sister said, "I want ringlets like Winnie's," and she said it in a very loud voice to show that she wouldn't fuss, so our mother didn't say anything else; and when Mrs Cocoa came over at my sister's bedtime, with a lot of strips of pink rag, and asked for my sister's hairbrush and a basin of water, our mother fetched them for her without saying a word about how my sister usually fussed.

Now, my sister had said that she wasn't going to be a naughty girl when Mrs Cocoa curled her hair, and she knew that Mother expected her to be naughty, so although she found that she didn't like having her hair twisted up into rags very much, she was good as gold.

My sister didn't like having her hair twisted up into those rags one bit. You see, her hair was rather long, and Mrs Cocoa had to twist and twist very tightly indeed to make sure that the curlers would stay in; and the tighter the curl-rags were the more uncomfortable they felt.

But my sister didn't say so. She sat very good and quiet and she thought about all those lovely Winnie-ringlets, and when Mrs Cocoa had finished she thanked her very nicely indeed and went upstairs with Rosy-primrose, with her hair all curled up tight with little pink rags sticking up all over her head.

But, oh dear.

Have *you* ever tried to sleep with curlers in *your* hair? My sister tried and tried, but wherever she turned her head there was a little knob of hair to lie on and it was most uncomfortable.

She tried to go to sleep with her nose in the pillow but that was most feathery and unpleasant.

In the end the poor child went to sleep with her head right over the edge of the bed and her arm tight round the bedpost to keep her from falling out.

That wasn't comfortable either, so she woke up.

When my little sister woke up she shouted because she couldn't remember why she was lying in such a funny way, and our mother had to come in to her.

When Mother saw how hard it was for my little sister to sleep with her curlers in, she said perhaps they had better come out, and that made my naughty little sister cry because she did want Winnie-ringlets, until Mother said, "Well, if you want curls don't fuss then," and went back to her own bed.

After that my poor sister slept and woke up and slept and woke up all night, but she didn't shout any more, and when morning came she was sleepy and cross and peepy-eyed.

But when she had had her breakfast, Mrs Cocoa came in to undo the curlers, and my sister cheered up and began to smile.

She sat very still while kind Mrs Cocoa took out the rags and carefully combed each ringlet into shape, and when Mrs Cocoa had finished, and my sister climbed up to see herself in the mirror, she smiled like anything.

And I smiled and Mother smiled.

She was a curly girl – curlier than Winnie even, because she had a lot more hair than Winnie had. She had real ringlets that you could push your fingers into!

My sister was a proud girl that day; she sat about in a still quiet way – just like Winnie did, and after dinner she fell fast asleep in her chair.

When my sister woke up she sat for a little while and did a lot of thinking, then she got down from her chair and went round to see Mrs Cocoa.

"Thank you very much, Mrs Cocoa, for making me a curly girl," my sister said, "but I don't think I will be curly any more. It makes me too sleepy to be curly."

"I know why Winnie is so quiet now," my sister said, "it's because she can't sleep for curlers. I think I would rather be me, fast asleep with pigtails."

And Mrs Cocoa said, "That's a very good idea, I think. Anyway, who wants *you* to look like that Winnie?"

10. My naughty little sister cuts out

Once, when I was a little girl, and my naughty little sister was a very little girl, it rained and rained and rained. It rained every day, and it rained all the time, and everything got wetter and wetter and wetter, and when my naughty little sister went out she had to wear her mackintosh and her wellingtons.

My naughty little sister had a beautiful red mackintosh-cape with a hood – just like Little Red Riding Hood's – and she had a little red umbrella. My little sister used to carry her umbrella under her cape, because she didn't want it to get wet. Wasn't she a silly girl?

When my naughty little sister went down the road, the rain went plop, plop, plop, plop, on to her head, and scatter-scatter-scatter against her cape, and trickle, trickle down her cheeks, and her wellington boots went splish-splosh, splish-splosh in the puddles.

My naughty little sister liked puddles very much, and she splished and sploshed such a lot that the water got into the tops of her wellingtons and made her feet wet inside, and then my naughty little sister was very sorry, because she caught a cold.

She got a nasty, sneezy, atishoo-y cold, and couldn't go out in the rain any more. My poor little sister looked very miserable when my mother said she could not go out. But her cold was very bad, and she had a red nose, and red eyes, and a nasty buzzy ear – all because of getting her feet wet, and every now and again – she couldn't help it – she said, "A-a-tishoo!"

Now, my naughty little sister was a fidgety child. She wouldn't sit down quietly to hear a story like you do, or play nicely with a toy, or draw pictures with a pencil – she just fidgeted and wriggled and grumbled all the time, and said, "Want to go out in the rain – want to splash and splash," in the crossest and growliest voice, and then she said, "A-a-tishoo!" even when she didn't want to, because of the nasty cold she'd got. And she grumbled and grumbled and grumbled.

My mother made her orange-drink, but she grumbled. My mother gave her cough-stuff, but she grumbled, and

really no one knew how to make her good.

My mother said, "Why don't you look at a picture-book?"

And my naughty little sister said, "No book, nasty book."

Then my mother said, "Well, would you like to play with my button-box?" and my naughty little sister said she thought she might like that. But when she had dropped all the buttons out and spilled them all over the floor, she said, "No buttons, tired of buttons. A-a-tishoo!" She said, "A-a-tishoo" like that, because she couldn't help it.

My mother said, "Dear me, what can I do for the child?"

Then my mother had a good idea. She said, "I know,

you can make a scrap-book!"

So my mother found a big book with clean pages, and a lot of old birthday cards and Christmas cards, and some old picture-books, and a big pot of sticky paste and she showed my naughty little sister how to make a scrap-book.

My naughty little sister was quite pleased, because she had never been allowed to use scissors before, and these were the nice snippy ones from mother's work-box.

My naughty little sister cut out a picture of a cow, and a basket with roses in, and a lady in a red dress, and a house and a squirrel, and she stuck them all in the big book with the sticky paste, and then she laughed and laughed.

Do you know why she laughed? She laughed because she had stuck them all in the book in a funny way. She stuck the lady in first, and then she put the basket of roses on the lady's head, and the cow on top of that, and then she put the house and the squirrel under the lady's feet. My naughty little sister thought that the lady looked very funny with the basket of flowers and the cow on her head.

So my naughty little sister amused herself for quite a long while, and my mother said, "Thank goodness," and went upstairs to tidy the bedrooms, as my naughty little sister wasn't grumbling any more.

But that naughty child soon got tired of the scrap-book, and when she got tired of it, she started rubbing the sticky paste over the table, and made the table all gummy. Wasn't that nasty of her?

Then she poked the scissors into the birthday cards and the Christmas cards, and made them look very ugly, and then, because she liked to do snip-snipping with the scissors, she looked round for something big to cut.

Fancy looking round for mischief like that! But she did. She didn't care at all, she just looked round for something to cut.

She snipped up all father's newspaper with the scissors, and she tried to snip the pussy-cat's tail, only pussy put her back up and said, "Pss," and frightened my naughty little sister.

So my naughty little sister looked round for something that she could cut up easily, and she found a big brown-paper parcel on a chair – a parcel all tied up with white string.

My naughty sister was so bad because she couldn't go out and play in the wet that she cut the string of the parcel. She knew that she shouldn't, but she didn't care a bit. She cut the string right through, and pulled it all off. She did that because she thought it would be nice to cut up all the

brown paper that was round the parcel.

So she dragged the parcel on to the floor, and began to pull off the brown paper. But when the brown paper was off, my very naughty little sister found something inside that she thought would be much nicer to cut. It was a lovely piece of silky, rustly material with little flowers all over it – the sort of special stuff that party-dresses are made of.

Now my naughty little sister knew that she mustn't cut stuff like that, but she didn't care. She thought she would just make a quick snip to see how it sounded when it was cut. So she did make a snip, and the stuff went "scc-scrr-scrr" as the scissors bit it, and my naughty little sister was so pleased that she forgot about everything else, and just cut and cut.

And then, all of a sudden . . . yes!

In came my mother!

My mother was cross when she saw the sticky table, and the cut-up newspaper, but when she looked on the floor and saw my naughty little sister cutting the silky stuff, she was very, very angry.

"You are a bad, bad child," my mother said. "You shall not have the scissors any more. Your kind Aunt Betty is going to be married soon, and she sent this nice stuff for me to make you a bridesmaid's dress, because she wanted you to hold up her dress in church for her. Now you won't be able to go."

My naughty little sister cried and cried because she wanted to be a bridesmaid and because she liked to have new dresses very much. But it was no use, because the stuff was all cut up.

After that my naughty little sister tried to be a good girl until her cold was better.

11. My naughty little sister and the workmen

My naughty little sister was a very, very inquisitive child. She was always looking and peeping into things that didn't belong to her. She used to open other people's cupboards and boxes just to find out what was inside.

Aren't you glad you aren't inquisitive like that?

Well now, one day a lot of workmen came to dig up all the roads near our house, and my little sister was very interested in them. They were very nice men, but some of them had rather loud shouty voices sometimes. There were shovelling men, and picking men, and men with jumping-about things that went, 'Ah-ah-ah-ah-ah-ah-aha-aaa,' and men who drank tea out of jam-pots, and men who cooked sausages over fires, and there was an old, old man who sat up all night when the other men had gone home, and who had lots of coats and scarves to keep him warm.

There were lots of things for my little inquisitive sister to see: there were heaps of earth, and red lanterns for the old, old man to light at night-time, and long pole-y things to keep people from falling down the holes in the road, and workmen's huts, and many other things.

When the workmen were in our road, my little sister used to watch them every day. She used to lean over the gate and stare and stare, but when they went off to the next road she didn't see so much of them.

Well now, I will tell you about the inquisitive thing my naughty little sister did one day, shall I?

Yes. Well, do you remember Bad Harry who was my little sister's best boy-friend? Do you? I thought you did. Now this Bad Harry came one day to ask my mother if my little sister could go round to his house to play with him, and as Bad Harry's house wasn't far away, and as there were no roads to cross, my mother said my little sister could go.

So my little sister put on her hat and her coat, and her scarf and her gloves, because it was a cold nasty day, and went off with her best boy-friend to play with him.

They hurried along like good children until they came to the workmen in the next road, and then they went slow as slow, because there were so many things to see. They looked at this, and at that, and when they got past the workmen they found a very curious thing.

By the road there was a tall hedge, and under the tall hedge there was a mackintoshy bundle.

Now this mackintoshy bundle hadn't anything to do with Bad Harry, and it hadn't anything to do with my naughty little sister; yet do you know they were so inquisitive that they stopped and looked at it.

They had such a good look at it that they had to get right under the hedge to see, and when they got very near it they found it was an old mackintosh wrapped round something or other inside.

Weren't they naughty? They should have gone straight home to Bad Harry's mother's house, shouldn't they? But they didn't. They stayed and looked at the mackintoshy bundle.

And they opened it. They really truly did. It wasn't their bundle, but they opened it wide under the hedge, and do you know what was inside it? I know you aren't an inquisitive meddlesome child, but would you like to know?

Well, inside the bundle there were lots and lots of parcels and packages tied up in red handkerchiefs, and brown paper, and newspaper, and instead of putting them back again like nice children, those little horrors started to open all those parcels, and inside those parcels there were lots of things to eat!

There were sandwiches, and cakes and meat-pies and cold cooked fish, and eggs, and goodness knows what-all.

Weren't those bad children surprised? They couldn't think how all those sandwiches and things could have got into that old mackintosh.

Then Bad Harry said, "Shall we eat some?" You remember he was a greedy lad. But my little sister said, "No, it's picked-up food." My little sister knew that my mother had told her never, never to eat picked-up food. You see she was good about *that*.

Only she was very bad after, because she said, "I know,

let's play with it."

So they took out all those sandwiches and cakes, and meat-pies and cold cooked fish and eggs, and they laid them out across the path and made them into pretty patterns on the ground. Then Bad Harry threw a sandwich at my little sister and she threw a meat-pie at him, and they began to have a lovely game.

And then, do you know what happened? A big roary voice called out, "What are you doing with our dinners, you monkeys – you?" And there was a big workman coming towards them, looking so cross and angry that those two bad children screamed and screamed, and because the workman was so roary they turned and ran and ran back down the road, and the big workman ran after them as cross as cross. Weren't they frightened?

When they got back to where the other roadmen were digging, those children were more frightened than ever, because the big workman shouted to all the other workmen all about what those naughty children had done with their dinners.

Yes, those poor workmen had put all their dinners under the hedge in the old mackintosh to keep them dry and safe until dinner-time. As well as being frightened, Bad Harry and my naughty little sister were very ashamed.

They were so ashamed that they did a most silly thing. When they heard the big workman telling the others about their dinners, those silly children ran and hid themselves in one of the pipes that the workmen were putting in the road.

My naughty little sister went first, and old Bad Harry after her. Because my naughty little sister was so frightened she wriggled in and in the pipe, and Bad Harry came wriggling after her, because he was frightened too.

And then a dreadful thing happened to my naughty little sister. That Bad Harry *stuck in the pipe* – and he couldn't get any farther. He was quite a round fat boy, you see, and he stuck fast as fast in the pipe.

Then didn't those sillies howl and howl!

My little sister howled because she didn't want to go on and on down the roadmen's pipes on her own, and Bad

Harry howled because he couldn't move at all.

It was all terrible, of course, but the roary workman rescued them very quickly. He couldn't reach Bad Harry with his arm, but he got a long hooky iron thing, and he hooked it in Bad Harry's belt, and he pulled and pulled, and presently he pulled Bad Harry out of the pipe. Wasn't it a good thing they had the hooky iron? And wasn't it a *very* good thing that Bad Harry had a strong belt on his coat?

When Bad Harry was out, my little sister wriggled back and back, and came out too, and when she saw all the poor workmen who wouldn't have any dinner, she cried and cried, and she told them what a sorry girl she was. She told the workmen that she and Bad Harry hadn't known the mackintoshy bundle was their dinners, and Bad Harry said he was sorry too, and they were so really truly ashamed that the big workman said, "Well, never mind this time. It's pay-day today, so we can send the boy for fish and chips instead," and he told my little sister not to cry any more.

So my little sister stopped crying, and she and Bad Harry both said they would never, never meddle and be inquisitive again.

12. The cross, spotty child

One day my naughty little sister wasn't at all a well girl.
She was all burny and tickly and tired and sad and spotty,
and when our nice doctor came to see her he said, "You've
got measles, old lady."

"You've got measles," that nice doctor said, "and you
will have to stay in bed for a few days."

When my sister heard that she had measles she began to
cry, "I don't want measles. Nasty measles," and made
herself burnier and ticklier and sadder than ever.

Have you had measles? Have you? If you have you will
remember how nasty it is. I am sure that if you did have
measles at any time you would be a very good child. You
wouldn't fuss and fuss. But my sister did, I'm sorry to say.

She fidgeted and fidgeted and fussed and cried and had
to be read to all the time, and wouldn't drink her

orange-juice and lost her hanky in the bed until our mother said, "Oh dear, I don't want you to have measles, I'm sure."

She *was* a cross, spotty child.

When our mother had to go out to do her shopping, kind Mrs Cocoa Jones came in to sit with my sister. Mrs Cocoa brought her knitting with her, and sat by my sister's bed and knitted and knitted. Mrs Cocoa was a kind lady and when my little sister moaned and grumbled she said, "There, there, duckie," in a very kind way.

My little sister didn't like Mrs Cocoa saying "There, there, duckie" to her, because she was feeling cross herself, so she pulled the sheet over her face and said, "Go away, Mrs Cocoa."

But Mrs Cocoa didn't go away; she just went on knitting and knitting until my naughty little sister pulled the sheet down from her face to see what Mrs Cocoa could be doing and whether she had made her cross.

But kind Mrs Cocoa wasn't cross – she was just sorry to see my poor spotty sister, and when she saw my sister looking at her, she said, "Now, I was just thinking. I believe I have the very thing to cheer you up."

My sister was surprised when Mrs Cocoa said this instead of being cross with her for saying "Go away" so

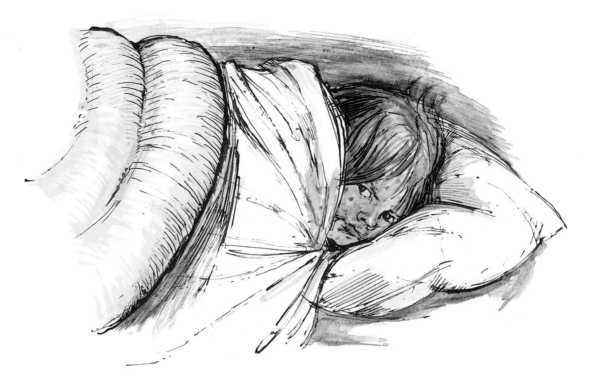

she listened hard and forgot to be miserable.

"When I was a little girl," Mrs Cocoa said, "my granny didn't like to see poor not-well children looking miserable, so she made a get-better box that she used to lend to all her grandchildren when they were ill."

Mrs Cocoa said, "My granny kept this box on top of her dresser, and when she found anything that she thought might amuse a not-well child she would put it in her box."

Mrs Cocoa said that it was a great treat to borrow the get-better box because although you knew some of the things that would be in it, there was always something fresh.

My little sister stopped being cross and moany while she listened to Mrs Cocoa, because she hadn't heard of a get-better box before.

She said, "What things, Mrs Cocoa? What was in the box?"

"All kinds of things," Mrs Cocoa said.

"Tell me! Tell me!" said my spotty little sister and she began to look cross because she wanted to know so much.

But Mrs Cocoa said, "I won't tell you, for you can see for yourself."

Mrs Cocoa said, "I hadn't thought about it until just this very minute; but do you know, I've got my granny's very own get-better box in my house and I had forgotten all about it! It's up in an old trunk in the spare bedroom. There are a lot of heavy boxes on top of the trunk, but if you are a good girl now, I will ask Mr Cocoa to get them down for me when he comes home from work. I will get the box out of the trunk and bring it in for you to see tomorrow."

Wasn't that a beautiful idea?

Mrs Cocoa Jones said, "I haven't seen that box for years and years, it will be quite a treat to look in it again. I am sure it will be just the thing to lend to a cross little spotty girl with measles, don't you?"

And my naughty little sister thought it *was* just the thing indeed!

So, next morning, as soon as my sister had had some bread and milk and a spoonful of medicine, Mrs Cocoa came upstairs to see her, with her grandmother's get-better box under her arm.

There was a *smiling* spotty child waiting for her today.

It was a beautiful-looking box, because Mrs Cocoa's old grandmother had stuck beautiful pieces of wallpaper on the lid and on the sides of the box, and Mrs Cocoa said that the wallpaper on the front was some that had been in her granny's front bedroom, and that on the back had been in her parlour. The paper on the lid had come from her Aunty Kitty's sitting-room; the paper on one side had been in Mrs Cocoa's mother's kitchen, while the paper on the other side which was really lovely, with roses and green dicky-birds, had come from Mrs Cocoa's own bedroom wallpaper when she was a little girl!

My sister was so interested to hear this that she almost forgot about opening the box!

But she did open it, and she found so many things that I can only tell you about some of them.

On top of the box she found a lovely piece of shining stuff folded very tidily, and when she opened it out on her bed she saw that it was covered with round sparkly things that Mrs Cocoa said were called spangles. Mrs Cocoa said that it was part of a dress that a real fairy queen had worn in a real pantomime. She said that a lady who had worked in a theatre had given it to her grandmother long, long ago.

Under the sparkly stuff were boxes and boxes. Tiny boxes with pretty pictures painted on the lids, and in every box a nice little interesting thing. A string of tiny beads, or a little-little dollie, or some shells. In one box was a very little paper fan, and in another there was a little laughing clown's face cut out of paper that Mrs Cocoa's granny had stuck there as a surprise.

My sister was so surprised that she smiled, and Mrs Cocoa told her that her granny had put that in to make a not-well child be surprised and smile. She said that she remembered smiling at that box when she was a little girl. Mrs Cocoa's old granny had been very clever, hadn't she?

There were picture postcards in that not-well box, and pretty stones – some sparkly and some with holes in them. There was a small hard fir cone, and pieces of coloured glass that you could hold up before your eyes and look through. There was a silver pencil with a hole in the handle that you could look through too and see a magic picture. There was a small book with pictures in it – oh, I can't remember what else!

It amused and amused my sister.

She took all the things out carefully and then she put

them all back carefully. She shut the lid and looked at the wallpaper outside all over again.

Then she took the things out again, and looked at them again and played with them and was as interested as could be!

And Mrs Cocoa said, "Well, I never! That's just what I did myself when I was a child!"

When my sister was better she gave the box back to Mrs Cocoa – just as Mrs Cocoa had given the box back to her granny.

Mrs Cocoa Jones laid all the things from the box out in the sunshine in her back garden to air them after the measles. She said her grandmother always did that, and because Mrs Cocoa's granny had done it, it made it all very specially nice for my little sister to think about.

After that, my sister often played at making a get-better box with a boot-box that Mother gave her, and once she drew red chalk spots on poor Rosy-primrose's face so that she could have measles and the get-better box to play with.